"Look Adonis, she wants more than a little room service. I see you're a married man. You have a better chance of to get her to step off than I would okay. I will gladly hold down the front desk for you but if you don't mind can you go up instead, just this once?" Terrell pleaded.

"Okay, it's not like we haven't had a lonely guest or two before. I'll handle her. Don't worry though, you will get used to it. Is that how you got that make-up on your shirt?" Adonis asked.

Terrell nodded yes.

"Well I hate to be the one to tell you, but you have some on your zipper too. Had enough?" Adonis joked.

© *Inakat* 2012

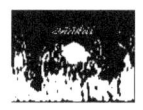

Inakat Publishing Detroit, Michigan

ISBN # 978-0-9883533-2-9

Library of Congress Control Number: 2012953165

Cover Design By: © Inakat Graphic Designs

Dedication

As always to my family, I love you.

"You will always be the wind beneath my wings"

Speak softly and carry a big stick; you will go far."

African Proverb

As cited

By President Theodore Roosevelt

Chapter 1 - Stiletto Seduction

When Adonis saw Chelae come into the hotel with Kristen he'd paid her little attention at first. Many guests came and went every day. He'd come from behind the counter to see if he could help with their bags. Chelae rifled through her purse to try and find her reservation slip. In the process, a pack of her business cards hit the floor.

Adonis bent down to return them to her. He stayed hunched over a little too long. His eyes slowly traveled up from the heel of her stiletto and stopped at her eyes as he rose. He swallowed hard, and then shoved the cards at her chest. Adonis nearly touched her bosom.

Kristen stared at him and then cleared her throat. Adonis smiled and stepped back before he offered Chelae help with their bags. Kristen face flushed, she'd known she'd no right to expect anything from Chelae, yet it irritated her when someone else had shown her attention or interest.

Afterwards, he scurried back behind the desk and kept his eyes glued to the computer screen as he went over her reservations. Adonis asked Chelae for identification, before he turned over two sets of keys for the rooms. She reached in the side pocket of her purse and passed him her driver's license. He looked at it and gave it back.

"Is there a price difference for the other room sir? I can pay for that now." Chelae offered.

"If there are any additional charges, you can settle it at check out." Adonis said.

"That's fine."

"The porter will escort you to your room shortly."

"Thank you."

Chelae looked around the hotel lobby and admired the high-vaulted ceilings and huge crystal chandelier.

The floor was covered in dark grey high-traffic carpet. She was impressed at the cleanliness of the space and was glad she'd come.

When the porter sprinted towards Chelae and swooped up her bags, she was startled at his speed. The porter told the women to follow him and proceeded to head across the lobby to a set of elevators. Chelea and Kristen followed closely behind.

The young man pushed the up button for the elevator and the shiny silver slabs opened immediately. The women stepped inside the box and the porter followed with the luggage. He pushed the #3 while Chelae rifled through her purse to prepare a tip for him.

The elevator stopped on the third floor and the doors opened to an elegantly decorated hallway. As the trio exited, Chelae noticed that Oil Paintings hung along the walls the entire length of the hallway. The porter walked quickly with the bags, before he stopped at a door.

"Excuse ma'am but may I have the key?" He asked.

Chelae gave him both sets of keys and waited while he opened the door. The young man opened the door and flipped on the light switch. Kristen leaned over Chelae's shoulder and gasped. The hotel room had a spectacular view of the New York skyline with opened drapes that were meant to cover the glass doors. The doors led to a balcony that held two high back lounge chairs and an ashtray. Chelae rushed inside the room to get a closer look.

The porter waited patiently while she looked over the room. After Chelae had peeked out on the balcony, she then patted the bed and walked over to the closet. Then she headed for the bathroom and turned on the light. Finally satisfied that the room was in order, she turned to the porter and handed him a tip.

"Thank you. Now, whichever one of you is going to take the other room please follow me." He said.

Kristen rolled her eyes and grumbled. Chelae cocked her head to the side and placed her hand on her hips. The porter looked around the room as the exchange went on. At last Chelae spoke up.

"You can leave my things here; however, we will both be going to see the other room." Chelae said.

"Yeah, because she's a spoiled selfish diva and whichever room she thinks is best is the one she's keeping." Kristen said.

"Okay." The porter said.

Chelae pouted when she heard Kristen's statement. She lifted her head high in the air and clutched her purse strap tightly. Chelae refused to be pulled into argument with Kristen. The porter held the door open while the two women went out into the hall. Kristen stepped aside and swept her arm out for Chelae to go first.

The trio headed down to the second floor quietly. When they finally arrived to the door of the second room,

Kristen again stepped aside for Chelae to go first. Chelae smiled when the door swung open and Kristen and the porter followed her into the room.

"Well?" Kristen said.

The porter struggled to hold in his laughter. The rooms in the hotels on the second and third floor were basically the same, with the exception of the view. Chelae put her hands on her hips again and waited for Kristen to continue. Kristen was quiet.

"Well what?" Chelae asked.

"Bay, which one of the rooms do you want?" Kristen said.

"No, I'm a spoiled Diva remember? So which one do you want?" Chelae retorted.

"You're not going to let that go huh?" Kristen said.

"You started it." Chelae said.

"I'll stay here, if that's okay with you." Kristen said.

"Whatever." Chelae responded.

"That's settled then." The porter said.

The women turned towards him and stared. He began to shuffle nervously from one foot to the other. After a few awkward seconds of silence, the porter excused himself and left. The two women snickered as he left quickly.

Kristen had a habit to comment about Chelae's Diva traditions. Chelae had long grown accustomed to the quips from Kristen. In fact, Kristen had known from the start that Chelae was into herself. Nevertheless, a huge part of Kristen's constant attraction to Chelae was that she was high-maintenance. Kristen would remark to goad Chelae into an argument with her to get Chelae's attention. In the end Kristen always catered to Chelae's nuisances.

From the time the women had met, Kristen would spend hours as she watched Chelae get ready to go out. She loved the way she could wreck a closet. Chelae could take hours in the mirror as she tweezed, patted, primped, and moisturized. Chelae was addicted to the good-life for her and Kristen was her enabler.

Kristen loved to witness Chelae and was usually quite happy to be a part of her daily routine. She had her own personal motives to not want anyone else around Chelae. Kristen would be damned if someone else would get to enjoy the little details that she'd been privy to.

She found Chelae incredibly sexy when she was privileged enough to "accidently" wander into the bathroom while Chelae shaved her legs. The thought of her chocolaty legs, draped seductively over the edge of the tub, all lathered in cream had always turned Kristen on. Other intimate moments, such as the way Chelae applied her make-up seemed to be equally erotic to Kristen, especially when Chelae put lip gloss on her full lips.

There was a hands-off way of the two women had that was sexual and flirty. The relationship between the two was slightly odd; in the sense that while on the surface they appeared to antagonize one another. The truth was that Chelae enjoyed Kristen's attention as much as Kristen liked to give it. Whenever the other was interrupted from the torture of the other, they both quickly got upset with the intruder.

Kristen didn't mind Chelae quirky and sometimes needy nature, just as long as it was Kristen that she needed. To an outsider that looked in, the women appeared to hate each other enough to the point of just a push away from the edge of insanity. Chelae often found herself annoyed with Kristen. Nevertheless, she had found a need for her company at times.

"Fine then, I hope you sleep well in the bed alone. It's not like Marsha was going to take you anywhere but a cheap short stay at a seedy dump anyway." Chelae said.

"You didn't have to go there Chelae. Do you know that you can be an insufferable bitch sometimes?" Kristen said.

"You want a lick right now don't you?"

"Take your ass to your room, before I bend you over that nightstand and you leave this room crawling. You ought to try a wedge heel or flat shoes sometimes. Strutting around in them stilettoes all the time is going to get you in trouble. I know you doing that shit to get to me. Keep playing with me, you just keep on playing with me."

Chelae's eyes grew wide. She knew Kristen well enough to understand what that meant. She'd just gotten her hair done. Chelae wasn't anxious to spend the rest of her trip in New York with a Treasure Troll hair-do, after Kristen was done with her. Chelae did her best not to smile, as she eased back out the door. She feared Kristen might change her mind.

Chapter 2 - Adonis

The crisp morning air blew gently across Chelae's face roused her from a deep sleep. She sat up and slipped her feet into her soft fuzzy black slippers. This was her first night away from the city in a long time. She walked over to the hotel window and gently slid the glass closed.

The thick burgundy shag carpet complimented the soft cream walls. A large dark brown console cabinet hid away the television, while matched nightstands and a chest of drawers gave the room a home-like feel. The multicolored floral drapes added a vibrant splash of color, and blended well to make the room comfy and private.

The hotel itself was a change of pace from her usual trips. It was beautifully decorated around a California King bed. The room was a set up for a Diva with attitude all the way down the well-lit vanity. Chelae eased back onto the bed and reached for the telephone on the nightstand. She called down to the front desk.

"Your Seasons Hotel, Adonis speaking, how may I help you?"

"This is Chelae Thomas in room 313. I have a meeting scheduled this afternoon. I was wondering if there might be a conference room available this afternoon for viewing. I have to do a presentation soon. I'll need a projection screen." Chelae said.

"Hmm just give me a second and I'll check for you."

"Sure"

"Well, we have several rooms available. You can come down and take a look around."

"Will you be able to show me?"

"I'd be happy to."

Chela was permanently in the process to become a better person physically and mentally, but lately the goal had been professionally. She was usually a leader by example; however, she enjoyed that chance to do what she'd rarely done. Walk out on the ledge and take a risk on her. Chelae's original goal had been to go for the corner office in life. Then she'd decided she'd prefer her own building.

She had a strong sense of style and self-worth. The thorn in her side was she'd never been satisfied completely with who she was. Chelae felt she could always be better or work harder. At one point in her life she'd given in to workaholic behavior and left many personal ambitions to the side. Chelae hoped this trip would get her back on track.

Chelae had given Kristen a quick hug and went back to her to rest. The moment she'd entered the room. She stripped from her travel clothes down to her skivvies. Once Chelae's head hit the pillow she was fast asleep. She didn't wake until the next morning.

When she did wake, Chelae rolled off the bed and walked into the bathroom in front of the full length mirror, the sensor sparked on the lights and revealed her soft, shapely body. Chelae's short and petite stature hid the love-making animal she was.

She stood barely five feet tall and weighed one hundred thirty pounds; she had a pudgy nose, high cheeks bones, and full lips. She wore contacts and had a small scar above and a slight laziness in her left eye. Chelae liked to wear her hair in various styles for flexibility. She glanced back at the bed once more, and fought the urge to nestle her tiny body back under the warm blanket.

Chelae brushed her hands over her tummy and then she glanced back at the bed one final time. Still Chelae struggled with the temptation go back to sleep. She realized that she hadn't spoken to Kristen yet. She'd come on the trip with her for moral support. Chelae imagined Kristen was still in her room fast asleep.

They'd once been lovers. The affair had long turned from a passion filled romance to a casual acquaintance. As she looked at herself in the mirror she wished it was Kristen's hand on her midsection, in place of her own.

Chapter 3 - Fuel

Kristen and Chelae were worlds apart, in the sense that Kristen didn't seem to trust her own decisions. She was married with four children. Kristen had told Chelae that she'd gotten married because that's what was expected of her. When Kristen and Chelae met it was a clash of lust versus pure freak. While Kristen wasn't always sure what she should think and her moods changed from moment to moment, it was clear that she did want Chelae.

Chelae tended to be more responsible and had volunteered to be the person that kept Kristen grounded. As long as they were a couple. After the break-up, Chelae had made of point to simply remain her friend. She'd learned to feed Kristen with a long-handled spoon and let her tend to her own affairs.

Chelae had issues. Although she was beautiful and intelligent, she fought constantly with her own self-worth. Chelae spent a great deal of time working on her inner-self in private. She'd never manage to overcome the way she'd viewed herself as a work in progress versus a complete person after being molested. Chelae had feared that her sexuality had caused her to the victim of choice for her attacker.

Kristen was five foot four, with a light mocha complexion, and carried a few extra pounds in her mid-section. Kristen had been a heavy drinker who'd begun to let her appearance go. She said that she'd grown up in near poverty and that it had made Kristen a tough individual. She cared little about her style of dress, just so long as her clothes matched.

Chelae found Kristen very hard to understand completely. Kristen was in the process to find her as well. Kristen could associate easily with others, but shied away from personal conversations about her. Kristen was a heavy drinker as well. Chelae suspected that Kristen's drinking had to do with dealing with a painful childhood.

Chelae was a rape survivor. In her early teens, her sexual identity began to emerge when she'd shown a preference for the soft gentle touch of a woman. She eventually tired of questions about her "boyfriend"; she'd decided to try her hand in the men department. However, when it came down to the sex game, she couldn't shake the demons from her rape. After Chelae was done sexually, she wanted the man to go home or at least away from her, which she attributed to the rape.

Her relationship with David was an attempt to "stand by her man". She'd met him at the market several months after she had decided that she and Kristen were a thing of the past. Chelae hated to admit it, but she thought of him as the male version of Kristen. After the first few months, the similarities were hard to ignore. His mouth and unwarranted cockiness had begun to grate her last nerve.

Chelae had never cared for his comments about things that concerned her femininity. Such as her nails or hair, he didn't offer to pay for upkeep, but was quick to dish out advice. Whenever he'd brought her what were to be small tokens of affections, he bragged about it so much that she began to refuse his gifts.

At last, he'd become angry and hostile and then begun to accused her of another lover. Chelae ignored him. He'd spent plenty of time to make snide comments and very little effort to encourage her. In contrast to Kristen, who actually flirted when she remarked.

David had been so arrogant, that he hadn't realized that she didn't collapse from broken hearted pain. It was the final relief from the tremendous weight of their tryst had ended. Chelae had begun to despise him. Especially, when she found that he preened like a peacock in front of other women. Even though she known he was the "pillow princess" in bed. Chelae had only slept with him once the entire time, mainly because of a lack of trust with him.

Chelae was usually bright and smooth-spoken, able to focus energy on a single problem until it's solved. She was perceptive, intelligent, knowledgeable and very skillful in a bed. She had been confident anything was possible, if she could focus all energy and concentrated thought on it. She'd strived to become an expert in her field. However, she'd wasn't friendly but looked inward for answers, always deep in thought. The episode with David had her left her feeling a little less than her usual stellar self.

She was concerned with her appearance most of the time, yet she wasn't beyond a simple dress with little make-up. At first glance, she appeared subservient, laid-back, and at times withdrawn. Chelae was most comfortable in her mind to work on problems.

She was actually imaginative and could charm to others when it was called for. Chelae had a quiet kind of appeal that drew others to her, while a raw sexual energy always lurked just under her skin. That energy was usually reflected in her style of dress and demeanor.

Chelae worked as an Internet Securities Exchange Researcher. Her job required countless hours in front of a computer. When's she's wasn't on her laptop, her I-phone was close at hand. At work, Chelae was analytic and saw information as the lifeblood of business. She was able to combine information to make informed decisions. She was attracted to work where research was important.

Chelae and Kristen both appreciated their shared respect for boundaries most of the time. Still, when Chelae became private, Kristen had doubts and concerns about whether they would always have each other. Kristen became intrusive and accusatory. She wanted more support and involvement from Chelae. Chelae was pissed off at Kristen demands, while she still had a husband and children to attend to.

Chelae had told Kristen that she was irresponsible to have babies with a man she didn't really want to be with and inconsiderate towards her. The fact was Chelae was uncomfortable with the thought that Kristen might decide to work her marriage out and Chelae would wake up alone.

Chelae had fallen deeply in love with Kristen right off. She was determined that she would have some say-so about her hear when it came to how she'd dealt with Kristen or for that matter any lover. Should the day come that Kristen wanted to leave; Chelae hadn't planned to be the one on the floor.

Kristen wanted to keep Chelae as a lover when she wanted a woman and then leave. Chelae had wanted to see Kristen for some intimate time one night. Kristen had shown up to her apartment drunk and reeked of cheap perfume. Kristen didn't usually wear perfume and they'd begun to fight.

It'd escalated into a physical fight. When it was over, Chelae stormed into the bathroom and slammed the door. The house had grown quiet and Chelae assumed

Kristen had left. When Chelae opened the bathroom door she saw Kristen had stripped naked and was on her bed.

"What are you doing?" Chelae asked.

"Come finish what old girl started. She couldn't get me off anyway."

Chelae came out of the bathroom and sat on the bed next to her. She'd begin to lightly touch her slit. She found Kristin was soaked wet as she humped furiously at her fingers. Chelae stood up and slipped out of her clothes, turned and then slapped Kristen in the face. Kristen jumped up, clutched her cheek, and raced to put her clothes on.

Kristen began to vandalize Chelae's house and curse her out for the blow to her face. She threw and broke family heirlooms, turned over furniture, and destroyed Chelae's clothes. Chelae called it emotional quits from that moment.

Chelae wanted to forgive her, but she'd lost most of her bright outlook and respect for her. Once Chelae understood that she shared Kristen with a man, she nearly lost her mind, but other women were too far for her. Chelae had begun to openly date other people.

Chelae was raised in a tense household. She'd had her fill of drama as she'd grown up. Both her parents were consumed by one thing, for her mother it was music. For her dad it was money, neither parent had time to focus on her. She had to learn to fit into the family structure alone and rarely put her trust in anyone. Chelae didn't trust Kristen or David fully because of her the turmoil she'd witnessed first hand in between her scant knowledge of couples.

She'd despised whenever she'd been brought into arguments between her parents. She often felt as if she'd been pulled in to judge what was right or wrong between grown-ups. Each parent had a way to punish her if she agreed with other side. Chelae had learned early on to stand there and do nothing.

Too many times she'd felt she was a pawn to get back at the other parent. In the meantime they'd seemed to have forgotten that she needed their love and support. After a particularly loud match one night between her parents, Chelae interrupted them with a scream of her own.

"You two make marriage look like a prison sentence." Chelae screamed.

At that moment she'd gave up on demands from others about what her success level should be or how she'd get there. Throughout her life, she had been misinterpreted as eccentric and a little loopy, but, in fact, she sensed the world in close detail. She suffered intensely and knew pain. Chelae had developed a protective wall around her as a child and vowed to never let it go.

Chelae felt it'd be less hassle to call later and let Kristen sleep in. This trip was important to her and she wanted to be at her best. She finally turned on the shower and adjusted the temperature. She went to the closet and removed travel bag from the floor. Chelae had hung her business suits up the when she first arrived, so when it came time to be dressed, it would be easy.

Her bath, nevertheless, was almost a meticulously scheduled event. Chelae laid her bag and outfit on the bed. She went back to the tub to check the water temperature once more, before she unpacked her bag to get in. A small part of her wondered if Kristen was even still in bed as she let the warm water run over her hand.

Chelae went to get her carry-on duffel bag and sat on the bed with it.

"Let's see" she said to her.

Chelae rummaged through her bag and pulled out two fresh razors, Shea butter soap, her favorite bath set, a pumice stone, an Egyptian cotton towel, make-up case, and a silk green panty set. Her hand brushed a switch in her bag and the large black leather bag began to vibrate.

She turned it off and giggled at her naughty play thing. Chelae traveled with toys to keep her focused, whenever she was stressed. Her sexual passions were so intense at times that it could be seen in her eyes. She zipped her bag and gathered the items as she headed to the bathroom.

The whirlpool tub, equipped with spa jets that pulsed water beams, was a feature of her room she had planned to enjoy later in the evening. Chelae reached for the vanity light switch and flooded the room with a soft glow from the light. She laid her make-up case and toiletries on the counter and pulled the shower curtain door closed. She stood in front of the bathroom mirror.

She took a good long look at her body in the steamy glass. She wiped away the condensation from the mirror with her hand. Chelae smiled at what she saw. She was pleased at thirty nine years old that her breasts were perky and her bottom was still firm and round. It was a gracious gift that she hadn't planned on.

Chelae neatly lined up her items inside the shower ledge, before she hung her personal towel on the hook just inside the door. As soon as she stepped inside the tub, the warm water thumped at her nipples. She stepped up into the stream and began to wet her face. She had just lathered her body with a sexy Moscato Ice moisturizer gel.

The phone on the hotel nightstand began to ring. She ignored it and continued. The caller hung up and called right back. Chelae's cheeks puffed as she blew out air before she quickly rinsed off and pulled down her towel to cover up. She stepped from the tub and quickened her pace before she leaped across the bed to answer on the fourth ring.

"Hello"

"This is Adonis, I'm sorry to bother you; someone left a package for you at the front desk. Would you like for me to bring it up to you?"

"Ummm Yes. Thank you."

Chelae rushed around to find something suitable to put on. She decided to wait to put on her clothes and settled for a fluffy pink robe that she'd brought with her. Frustrated that she hadn't been able to enjoy her shower, Chelae did her best to smile. She slipped into the luxurious fabric and tied the satiny belt just as she heard a soft knock on her hotel door.

Chelae did her best to grin as she reached for the silver handle of the door. She paused as she felt a trickle of cool water run down between her breasts. Her tongue slid sensuously over her lips which was a nervous habit. When she opened the door, she gasped.

The man that stood on the other side of the door, with a medium sized box in his hands, was a sight for sore eyes. Adonis was tall, dark, and dressed impeccably in a midnight blue suit with a crisp white shirt and baby blue tie. His teeth glistened like pearls of perfection. A soft scent of Hugo Boss cologne hung delicately in the air.

Chelae swallowed as she reached for the package. When Adonis's hand touched hers, she felt her clitoris began to swell. Anxiously, she snatched the box from his hands and slammed the door. Her right hand clutched the top of her robe while she held the delivery in the other hand.

The room began to suddenly feel much smaller to her. Chelae realized she had shut the door in Adonis's face. Her cheeks began to burn with embarrassment at her rude behavior. Just as she leaned her head against the door, he knocked again. The sound seemed to echo around the room, as she reluctantly touched the door handle.

When she opened the door, Adonis stood there. This time with his arms crossed defiantly. He waited patiently and seemed amused at the flustered look on

Chelae's face. She cleared her throat and tried to look him in the eyes. Adonis had a slight grin on his face.

"I apologize, that was quite rude of me. If you could give me a moment I'll get a tip for you." Chelae said.

"That feeling scared you too?" Adonis asked.

"What? I don't know what you're talking about."

"When our hands touched, I got a jolt of electricity all over me. I know you felt it too."

"Oh ummm, must have been static from the carpet."

"I doubt it. Listen, what time will you be coming down because it's kind of slow right now. I'm ready for whatever, I mean whenever you are."

"I can be ready in about an hour or so."

"The least you could do is having something to eat with me, while we're at it, after slamming the door in my face and all."

"We'll see."

Chelae watched as Adonis nodded a curt goodbye. She peeked down the hall and watched him swagger with pride down the hall. His broad shoulders rippled through the fabric of his suit. Chelae sighed.

Chapter 4 - Tokens

Chelae closed the door and flipped over the small brown box Adonis had delivered. She couldn't believe that she gave him a "call me maybe?" look and he let it go at that. It was a little hard to admit to her, that the problem to find love had more to do with her choices than bad luck. She turned her attention back to the box and opened it.

Chelae walked over to the bed and dumped the contents on the bed. A dark red jewel encrusted in a gold setting bounced off and hit the carpet. She bent down to get it. With the jewel in hand she sat on the edge of the bed and flipped it over in her hand.

She picked up the box curiously; Chelae searched for a return label on the box but found none. She peeked inside and noticed a small card and a black crush velvet string. The front of the card had a picture of a woman that wore the piece as a choker. Chelae took the material and put the jewel on it. Chelae pushed the box further on the bed, she opened the card.

"I still can't help but wait until you see that with me it's not the same." Love always, Thess.

Chelae smiled. She jumped up to try it on in the bathroom mirror. Thess had been a longtime friend turned lover from many years ago. Most of the time, she'd known just what to say or do to bring her spirits up, today was no exception.

The history between them had been a passionate storm. They'd only met at Thess's insistence, over a decade past. Chela was in a new relationship with Kristen and Thess had dated a stripper. Chelae had found Thess attentive, intelligent, and easy to talk to. They'd met on a phone line and had been buddies of a sort ever since.

Their conversations had ranged from grocery prices to kids. Almost daily, they'd begun to call each other about everything in their lives. The bond in the search for love in all the wrong places was one they shared. After eight months of phone conversations, Thess called Chelae later than usual one night.

When she saw Thess's house number on her caller ID, she panicked. Immediately she thought it rather odd. Thess worked late. Her routine had been to go home, shower and sleep. Chelae was the first call she made in the mornings. She snatched the phone up.

"Hey, what's wrong?"

"Did I wake you? Nothing wrong, I just wanted to hear your voice. I had a crappy day at work."

"What happened?"

"I kept making mistakes and getting frustrated."

"Is it what's going on with your girl or just a bad day?"

"Both. I'm sick of coming home to an empty bed, while she's out doing whatever."

"Its 3:00 in the morning, she's not home yet?"

"No. I work hard. I deserve so much more. Chelae what am I doing wrong? You're a femme, so please help a brother out."

"Thess, I wish I knew. My girl ain't here either. It's messed up that I haven't seen her in two days, so I understand. It sucks to give your love to someone who seems like they don't care. Is that what made your day crappy at work too?"

"No, I couldn't stop thinking about how much I like talking to you. I kept trying to imagine what your face looked like. I was hoping you were alone tonight. Can I ask you a personal question?"

"Sure"

"Do you sleep with panties on?"

"Well, usually yes. Why?"

"Every ounce of me wants to come over there and slide them off of you right this instant."

"You don't even know what I look like. Your just upset now, I doubt that you want to do that."

"I do. Chelae are we ever going to meet?"

"Maybe, but I'm warning you, I'm ugly as sin."

"I don't care about that. You're beautiful inside and you've kept me from going insane for this past year. It would be so nice to have a face to go with the voice and mind."

"Look Thess, I'm overweight, buck-toothed, and knock-kneed, with a lazy eye. I love things the way they are now between us. I have a stud and you have a girl, we lean on each other for emotional support. I don't want to cross that line and lose my friendship with you."

"Nothing will change our friendship. Please, I've been asking for months now. You're over there alone and I'm over here by myself. It's not fair that they both get faithful partners and we can't even have a cup of coffee together. For all I know they are together now. Let's bet on it. If your girl doesn't come home by tomorrow night then we meet on Saturday."

"Alright."

Friday night came and went with no Kristen. The next Saturday brought a cheerful phone call from Thess. Chelae admitted right off that she'd lost the bet. Thess laughed as they made plans to hang out that afternoon.

Chelae had grown comfortable enough with talking to Thess to take her somewhere special. Her tummy crawled with butterflies as she gave her the address to her parents' house. She'd spent the day lazily preparing to meet up with Thess. She called her mother to let her know that an acquaintance wanted to drop by later. Chelae's mom giggled in the phone.

"You're bringing someone here? You must want my opinion. Let me tell you now I'll give my advice but I don't want any drama at my house. Did you break-up with that man's wife yet?" Her mom asked.

"Ma, why do you have to say it like that? I haven't seen her in nearly four days and this is not drama. We've been talking as friends for a while but for some reason I'm terrified to meet her alone. She's has a woman and I'm cool with that and she knows about Kristen. I'd appreciate some moral support and yes your opinion. I'm going to get it whether I ask or not."

"True. I'll see you in a while then."

"Thanks. I love you."

"I love you more."

Chelae got dressed and called Thess. Thess told Chelae that she was already on her way. Chelae called a cab and waited nervously. She hoped that Thess would forgive her. She was expected to meet a tall, heavy, woman with knock-knees, bucked teeth, and a lazy eye. In fact, Chelae was short, slim, and loved to wear stilettos. She'd chosen a snug black pant suit with a low-cut jacket, which showed her 38B cleavage.

Her hair was black with a crisp cut bang and flowed down to her shoulders. The City Girl perfume smelled like candy on her skin. She'd applied "Kiss me Back" lip gloss over a brown lip liner. Chelae had chosen to wear a tiny rhinestone pin in her hair, on the side.

When the cab blew its horn, she nearly ran through the closed-door. She managed to leave the house and slid into the vehicle. She'd given the driver directions. Ten minutes later Chelae found herself on her mother's porch afraid to go in. The huge wood framed house promised coziness inside and beckoned her to open the door, as the car sped off.

As soon as she pulled open the screen, a delicious aroma of Southern Fried chicken and yams called her closer. She walked through the foyer, careful not bump any of her mother's many what-not shelves that decorated the entrance. Chelae heard laughter come from the back of the house where the kitchen was. She followed the sounds of joy and scent of food to her mother's favorite place in the house. When she arrived at the kitchen door, she saw a petite well-dressed woman that sat with her back to the door. Her hair was a neatly faded, shiny, bundle of natural curls.

Chelae spoke. Thess stopped in the midst of a giggle and her body stiffened. She slid the chair she was seated in back and stood. When she turned towards Chelae, her mouth fell open and she held her breath as Thess extended her hand.

"Don't just stand there girl, say something." Her mother quipped.

She reached out to take Thess's hand. When Thess gripped her hand and pulled in her arms to embrace her, Chelae nearly melted as her panties became soaked almost instantly. While she inhaled her perfume, Thess wrapped her arms around Chelae's waist and rested her head in the hollow of her neck. A raw, animal-like, sexual energy filled the room. They hugged for nearly two minutes before Chelae's mother cleared her throat to remind them she was still in the room.

'"It's so nice to finally meet you." Thess said as she backed up.

"The pleasure is all mines."

"I knew you were lying about your looks."

"You never mentioned that you were so freaking gorgeous. I'm sorry I lied to you. I don't have an excuse. I wanted to discourage this face to face and believe me, I am really sorry. Most of the women I kick it with are just on a "looking for sex" tip and I just wanted to talk."

"Me too. Now that I've seen you, our conversations will be that much more special."

The three women sat at the kitchen table and chatted. Thess explained her family dynamics and military experiences. Chelae didn't say much. Her mother commented and asked questions, she showed interest about Thess's life. Her mother and Thess had hit it off well.

When the evening was over, the women hugged and agreed to talk on the phone later. Chelae kissed her Mom and left headed back to her own house. She'd barely opened the front door when she heard the phone ring. She dropped her handbag on the couch and went to answer it.

Chapter 5 - Quiet Storm

"Hey sexy, just making sure you got home safely." Thess said.

"Thank you and yes I did."

"So is there anything you want to know, now that we've met?"

"I don't know. I'm glad we finally saw each other. Is there anything you want to tell me?"

"Honestly? Now that we've met?"

"Yeah, honestly."

"It's only a matter of time before I make love to every inch of you."

Since Chelae had met Thess, she'd begun to think about her daily much differently than before. There was a strong chemistry between the two women. Thess had turned on a sleeping sexual giant in Chelae that she'd never known was in her. Her late night thoughts had begun to turn towards Thess.

Sunday seemed like an eternity as the day rolled on. The house phone rang several times, each time Chelae had hoped it was Thess. Finally, Thess called. It was late Sunday night.

"Hey, what's up with you?" Chelae asked.

"Nothing, thinking about you all day again."

"Same here how was your day at work?"

"It was alright; I wish you could get out and meet me for a drink."

"Where at?"

"Anywhere. Splash would be fine."

I'd love to, but I still have the kids."

"Aww c'mon now. I've met your mom. She'd be more than happy to watch the kids while you get out of the house for a while. I'll pay her if need be. Any word from your girl?"

"No."

"Damn. Look, call your mom and ask, if so I'll pick you all up, we can drop them off and keep it moving. No sense in us being alone tonight, especially when…."

"When what?'

"Just find out and call me back OK?"

Tears formed in Chelae eyes and she thought about where her official lover might be. She placed her hand over her lip to keep her composure. It had occurred to her that Thess was right. It was unfair that she was home alone while Kristen was more than likely in someone else's bed.

Even though she'd found Thess absolutely sexy, Chelae didn't think an affair of her own was the answer. Still there was a part of her that wanted to know what Thess was like in bed. She'd imagined her to be a cross in between sensual and aggressive from their phone conversations.

The reasons that she should allow Thess to have what she wanted were many. Chelae had hoped that Kristen would come to her senses and come home. She didn't believe that would ever really happen though. From the moment she'd met Thess, Chelae knew that she'd never share Thess with anyone if she was her stud.

Chelae had called her mom and asked if the kids could come over for a while. Her mother readily agreed. She raced around and packed essentials and pajamas for the children, just in case. She'd called Thess back when she was done and told her to come pick them up.

Chelae felt the frustration of being caught between two people already. Kristen could be mean spirited and hurtful with her words at times. Thess on the other hand had a way that made Chelae want to dissolve in her arms, but she could also be quite vicious at times. So far she hadn't been that way towards Chelae.

Thess had mentioned to that she didn't understand what Chelae had seen in Kristen to begin with. Chelae had wondered the same about Thess and her girl too. She'd shrugged it off as opposites attracts and thought little more of it. Chelae had enjoyed their conversations, except for the quips about her personal life.

Chelae hadn't bothered to explain to Thess how Kristen had made her feel in the beginning. They'd shared an intimacy that she hadn't known before. Kristen was the first person to give her multiple orgasms. Her denial of Kristen was Chelae's spiteful punishment that hurt them both. Chelae was confident that Kristen wasn't the only one that could bring her to tears with her skilled tongue.

Chelae had agreed to let Thess pick her up to play cards with her and some friends. She'd worn a skin-tight jean set with a black lace shirt underneath. She hoped the snugness of her outfit would give her a chance to stop any extra activity, if she'd found her alone with Thess. The time since they visited each other felt like infinity.

When they'd arrived at Thess's apartment, Chelae was impressed with the neatness of her flat. There was a place for things and most of them were in its proper place. Thess opened the door and led her to the kitchen, from what Chelae could see.

The bright, pristine room was already filled with other people. Thess introduced Chelae to her downstairs neighbor, Quanah, and her brother Cell and his girl Wanda. They exchanged pleasantries and agreed to play "Rise and Fly" Spades. Chelae felt a little self-conscious about her clothes, after she'd notice everyone else was dressed comfortably in loose tee-shirts and jeans or sweatpants.

Thess and Quanah teamed up and lost miserably to Cell and Chelae. His girlfriend Wanda mixed frozen Daiquiris as they played the first few hands. She passed the drinks out and roamed into the living room. A loud soulful Jeffrey Osborne crooned "I'm Only Human" from the speakers a few minutes later. Chelae began to miss possible books, as she glanced across the table at Thess.

A startling brash chime signaled it was eleven at night. Chelae checked her watch to be sure before she'd explained to Thess that it was time for her to go. Cell and Wanda quickly said their goodbyes and disappeared down the stairs into the night. Quanah excused her and slipped quietly out the back door to her own apartment. Chelae realized that she and Thess were alone.

Chelae helped push the chairs back to the table and grabbed her purse. She walked back down the hall to the living room to wait for Thess. Thess cleaned and dried the glasses that they'd used and cut off the kitchen light. She walked down the hall and up to Chelae.

Thess stood face to face with Chelae and wrapped her hands around her waist. Chelae gripped her purse strap tightly, while she fought the impulse to wrap her arms around Thess. The scent of Thess's cologne excited Chelae. Chelae seductively licked her lips.

"You're shaking." Thess said.

"I umm, I umm…"

"You what? Baby what's wrong?"

Chelae parted her lips slightly and leaned her head. She softly planted her lips on Thess's mouth. Flashes went off when Thess slipped her moist tongue between Chelae's full, luscious lips. They began to kiss with an uncontrolled, pent up hunger.

Thess tugged at Chelae's jacket and caused the buttons to pop open. She pushed Chelae against the wall and began to grind up against her. Chelae threw her leg up while she stood. Thess glided her hand over Chelae's thick mound instinctively the moment she'd had the access she'd desired. The heat from the Chelae's pussy even through her jeans, had instigated Thess to whimper, as she laid her head in her lace covered breasts.

Chapter Six - Guess Who's Back

After that night, the friendship between the women had been changed. There was a quiet sexual tension between the two of them at all times. They often remembered special occasions like birthdays and such. However, the relationship was strained. Even if a relationship together was the "perfect decision", neither woman wanted to be the first to take that step.

A green late-modeled Taurus wagon came to a screeching halt at the corner of the block. Kristen fumbled with the door handle while held on to her drink. She'd been gone for nearly a week. She jumped out of the car and slammed the door just as the car burned rubber into the night.

Kristen mumbled and shook her head. She'd expected there would be an awful fight between her and Chelae. She had steeled her nerve and fortified anger towards Chelae. Things wouldn't be like this if Marsha would let her have it and break it off for good. Kristen had always been a party animal and she'd be damned if a batch of kids, a mate, or a side thing, was going to change any of that.

Kristen had told Marsha about Chelae. She'd gone to great legnths to cover up her affair with Marsha. It was Chelae that Kristen had hoped would be there for her. One the one hand she'd thought Chelae was a fool for it, but on the other she thought it would provide her with a main woman for the rest of her life.

With all the fights and heartache between them, Kristen seemed to think of Chelae in some terms as her ride or die chick, based on the things she'd said about Chelae to others. Chelae thought of Kristen as someone she wanted to be with, but accepted that at best, it wouldn't be more than what it had been. It had taken a long time for Chelae to understand that as much as she'd wanted Kristen to be the one, which Kristen had given her the best that she'd had to offer a woman to begin with.

At times Kristen could be show love and complete concern, but somewhere just underneath it all, the desire to hurt Chelae and bring her down a notch or ten hid. Inside Kristen rage the epic "I hate that I ever loved you" syndrome. The more Chelae showed her affection or attention, the worst the hate surfaced. Chelae in turn had learned to deal with Kristen with a long handled spoon when it came to access to her love.

Kristen had met a woman named Marsha at a bar one night. The woman was the bartender and sent her and her friends' drinks. Marsha had flirted with Kristen several times, but Kristen blew her off. Then Marsha came at her with money.

Despite the rockiness of the relationship with Chelae. Kristen had openly expressed her fear that any day Chelae would pack up and simply walk away. Marsha seemed gullible enough to line up for a potential new-babies mama to Kristen. Whenever Chelae had decided to walk away, there needed to be someone there to help with the kids, take care of the house, and the occasional warm body to come home to a few nights a week.

Marsha came across as way more laid-back and had less demands than Chelae. At first she listened for hours on end while Kristen bitched about Chelae. Marsha openly disapproved of Chelae's diva-style as too self-centered. Then, Kristen moved on to how Chelae spent massive amounts of money on her and the kids. Marsha began to dig deep into what she'd earned to keep Kristen's pockets laced. Finally, Kristen gave her the heart-wrenching story about how much the kids despised Chelae.

The next thing Marsha knew, she became mother Kristen's children. It would be quite a while before She'd realized that not only had she'd been duped, but it was the main reason that Chelae hadn't bothered to make a scene.

She was perfectly fine with someone else to take care of the children, while she saw Kristen as she pleased and didn't have to commit.

Kristen had no intention of an end with Chelae though. She would have her for as long as Chelae allowed it. While Kristen led Marsha to believe that she was had a hard time financially, she's saved up Marsha's money and bought Chelae yet another diamond ring.

Kristen had told Marsha she'd had plans with friends for a few drinks. A few hours after she'd left Marsha, she tumbled up the stairs at Chelae's and sat on the cold concrete rail and expected the porch light to come on any minute. Based on their history, Chelae should run down the stairs and breathe her usual sigh of relief that Kristen was unharmed, before she lit into her with the accusations.

Kristen would deny every bit of it and give her yet another story about what happened. Chelae would listen and before she took her upstairs. Kristen would normally make-love to Chelae until she was senseless, then fall asleep with her arms wrapped around her waist the way she always did. In the morning, life would be fine again, Kristen reasoned.

Chelae had gotten wind of Marsha months prior to their break-up. Chelae had made the decision to ask Kristen to take the children and get a place for them. Chelae had hoped that what she'd thought about Kristen was true. That Marsha would end up the built in nanny and finance Kristen's habits, while she enjoyed her company whenever she felt like it.

Several minutes went by and Chelae didn't open the door. Kristen figured she was sleep and took out her key. When she opened the door the house was dark. She called out to Chelae several times, but got no answer. Slowly, she made her way upstairs to the bedroom and pushed the door open. The bed was empty and Chelae was nowhere to be found.

Kristen walked over to the unmade bed and put her hand on the sheet. The bed was cold. She flicked on her lamp and surveyed the room. There were several items of clothes strewn about. Kristen realized that Chelae had fussed over what to wear.

It was a habit of Chelae's, whenever she was about to get dressed. She would literally wreck the entire room to find the perfect shoes, handbag, belt, and other items. She usually made the bed up before she left the house.

Kristen sniffed. A soft candy-like sweet scent hung in the air. She looked around the room once again before she left it to head to the bathroom, down the hall. When she turned on the bathroom lights, she noticed a puddle of water on the floor near the tub.

Someone had showered recently and left the curtain on the wrong side of the tub. She opened the shower curtain and saw a bottle of City Girl perfume and Baby Oil that sat on the ledge. Kristen eyes narrowed into slits. It was nearly two am and Chelae had been predictable to a fault.

She didn't have many friends or outside associates that Kristen knew about. She was always home with her kids and did housework or prepared meals and such. The scene around her led Kristen to believe that she hadn't left because of some emergency with the children.

She relieved herself of some of the liquor that she'd consumed and went to the sink to wash her hands. Kristen leaned against the ceramic bowl and reached to turn the handles. She froze in her steps. A fresh razor lay on the edge of the sink.

As long as she'd known Chelae, she'd understood that Chela had an issue with body hair. Chelae despised it and kept every inch of her body hairless with the exception of her head. Kristen washed her hands and left the bathroom agitated.

Kristen went back to the bedroom and lay across the bed. The room whirled in her vision. Kristen reached up and grabbed Chelae's pillow and buried her face into it. She began to cry. She'd always dreaded that this day would come.

She believed she earned it for the way she'd treated Chelae. Still it didn't help the fact that even though she'd deserved just that, it still hurt like hell. Kristen believed Chelae had gone spend her night in someone else's arms. Her gut churned.

Kristen's body heaved as the moment she'd feared crept over her. Chelae had put up with a lot and somehow still managed to be there. Kristen wanted to tell her so badly at that moment that she'd take it all back if she could. The constant lies, the women, the hurt, the pain, and the lonely nights. Every fiber of her body told her it was too late for that now. There little to do but release some of the pain through her tears.

She wiped her face and looked up at the digital clock on their shared nightstand. It seemed to taunt her that it was now three fifty eight in the morning. She was exhausted as she flipped the pillow over and dozed off fitfully. Kristen's face was swollen and puffy.

It was a quarter after five in the morning, when Thess dropped Chelae off at home. Her red thong dangled from her jacket pocket. Thess reached over and cupped Chelae's chin and looked her in the eyes. Thess kissed her once more. Chelae shuddered as a gush of juice rolled from between her now swollen lips.

She slid out of the car and quietly closed the door. Chelae sprinted lightly as she made her way onto the porch. Once she opened the door, Thess pulled off and headed home. Except for some extremely heavy kisses and fondling the women had managed to stave off the intensity of their respective urges for the moment.

The ache in Chelae's body grew with every step towards the door. The scent of her heated arousal wafted delicately up to her nose. Her rigid nipples strained against their lace constraints and begged for a soft warm tongue to caress them in place of the material. The scent of Thess's cologne was lodged in Chelae's jacket as well.

Chelae choked back tears as Thess drove away. The desire to be taken and savored had turned into a beast-like hunger inside of her. Her inner woman was starved for the release that she'd only felt from the touch of a woman. It wasn't like it was any random person she'd picked out of a crowd.

For Chelae, she'd potentially let the love of her life leave on a ship headed nowhere. Without much more than a few scant kisses. She rammed her hand inside her purse to find her house key and a tissue. The snot was already pooled up inside her nostrils.

Chelae had planned to go in and shower again. Then either let the desire die down or handle it if she had too. A thin square edge had lodged itself between her forefinger and thumb. When she pulled the object from her purse and she smiled through her tears. Thess had slipped the Jeffrey Osborne CD in her purse.

Chelae had assured her in the car, that she would stay awake and wait for Thess's call to say she'd arrived back home safely. She walked up the stairs and halfway she halted. She was certain she'd turned off all the lights before she'd left, but the bathroom light burned brightly. Chelae felt her heart hammer as she realized that someone else had been in the house.

She slowly unzipped her purse and dug around in it in the dark. When she felt the cold comfort of her switchblade she wrapped her fingers around it tightly. She withdrew the sharp edge from her purse and pushed the button. A soft click was the only sound in the house besides the hum of the refrigerator downstairs.

She slipped off her heels and held the shiny steel blade out in front of her. Chelae stealthily made her way up the rest of the stairs in silence. When she made it to the bedroom and saw Kristen passed out across the bed, she sighed. Carefully, she eased inside the room and put her purse on the chest of drawers. She laid the open blade next to it.

Chelae unfastened her jeans once and squirmed out of them. Chelae pulled at her jacket sleeve and the house phone rang. Kristen woke up and reached for the phone. Chelae shoved her thong deep in her pocket. She used the restroom at Thess's house and removed them.

Chelae felt a lump in her throat. Kristen answered the phone and passed it to Chelae. Chelae took the receiver and answered quickly and kept her conversation brief. She hung up just and listened quietly. Kristen went off in a tirade of accusations of her sneaking off with a man.

Chelae didn't respond. Instead she left the room and went to bathroom to shower. Kristen trailed behind her and demanded that Chelae prove that she hadn't been with anyone.

Chapter Seven - If only you knew

Chelae felt the tingle of the tears welled in her eyes as she fingered the necklace. The pain brought her back to where she was. She bowed brought her hands to her lips and kissed them, while she gripped the shiny jewel.

The past had haunted her even though she tried to move on. Chelae hoped very few people would ever see the vulnerable side of her, after this trip. Since she couldn't enjoy the trip as planned with her ex-boyfriend, she decided to learn as much as she could while there. Adonis's invitation couldn't have come at a better time, because Chelae knew little about New York. It was nearly a.m. and she'd yet to get dressed and review her notes for her new game plan. Chelae had been lost in her daydreams of the past for nearly an hour.

She shook her head and thought how she usually had chosen her partners because of a particular quality. Chelae hated to date. Most of them had ended in disaster. She'd seemed to pick the same kind of mate over and over. Lovers that talked a good game, but in the end lacked the skills or means to follow through with their promises.

Chelae had already lived a life full of broken promises and even dealt with domestic violence. She was from Detroit but she traveled to find work and new clients for her business. This trip hadn't been planned for business though, it was meant to be a romantic get-away.

She had planned to take this trip with David. It was intended to be a surprise to him. Chelae had pre-paid the expenses months before. Until she found pictures of him with another female naked with him in his phone. Chelae believed she knew who the woman was, but it really didn't matter. She'd called Kristen at the last minute and asked her to come along instead.

Afterward he tried to tell her how much he loved her. She almost caved in, until he went in his pocket and produced a ring that she'd seen in the picture. It was a fake piece of custom jewelry that he had given to someone else. Chelae couldn't believe he actually took the ring back let alone offered it to her.

When she saw the photos it confirmed what she'd already began to suspect a few weeks earlier. Chelae called the number that the pictures had been sent from. The woman claimed that she'd slept with him several times. Chelae thought of the picture the woman had sent and wondered aloud if that's what happened to his lunch money out loud.

"He ain't buy shit for' me. I just wanted to do it. It ain't my fault if yo' man like running up in me."

"What, are you trying to say? You think somehow that makes you better than me?"

"I ain't trying to say a damn thing. We hooked up at the Riverfront; he started begging for some ass. I told him no and he asked me for a blow job. I told him I wasn't sucking his dick, but what's up? He was all in."

"Wow"

"What? Don't be judging me. Check yo man."

"No, I'm going to check myself. A couple of times."

"What that mean?"

"It means I'd rather enjoy a stroll across the glass floor, with a tray of chocolate chip cookies, while watching a monkey eat a banana, than worry about a man that probably gets less pretty pussy than I do. You love, are not a looker by any means."

She'd then remember the fight that she had with David before she left for New York. Chelae was pissed that David had such a childish attitude towards monogamy. Had she known that upfront, Chelae would have never dated him. She let his words bite one more time.

"I'm trying to understand what your problem is. Why do you always have to behave like that? I mean it was fine in the beginning. I could understand your anger. I feel like you're making a big deal out of nothing. So I slept with someone else, smoked a few fifty ones? It's not like you were a virgin when I met you. What did you think I was out doing that time of night anyway? You didn't act like you cared. "David said.

"So, it's come to this huh? I'm past the arguing with you. I've been through too much.

You know you're right. You deserve so much more than I could ever give you." Chelae said.

"I think you're being sensitive. I'm going through a lot right now. You don't think about me. You're always off chasing one of your latest so called ventures. Do you really think that makes you special? If you think because you don't want to be freaky for your man, that I'm supposed to stop liking sex? What am I supposed to do book an appointment to see you?"

"I think you've done enough."

"Look baby, I'm going to give you a chance to calm down and adjust yourself. We can talk about it later. Give me some time to think about it. I think you need to spend more time trying to figure out how to keep your man happy. You don't even know that I slept with her. You just falling all to pieces about what she said, she could be telling you what you wanted to hear."'

"Oh, I'm adjusted and according to you blind as bat too. I'm going out to get some air; it's a little too stuffy in here. I'm think I'm choking on the scent of bullshit and toilet water perfume."

She'd felt anxious. Chelae turned and headed for the door and felt the first prickle as the tears rolled up. However, he had put their relationship into perspective for her. She'd decided that when he left for work, then she would pack her bags and leave for New York. Whenever he'd finally decided to come home, he'd figure it out. His car had barely left the driveway the next day, before she'd called Kristen and asked her to come along for company.

Chelae walked over to the hotel closet and rummaged through her suits. She found a floral print black dress. She wasn't sure what had hurt the most, the affair or his attitude about it. Kristen had already taken her through a broken heart mess.

None of that mattered now that she was single again. Chelae refused to take anyone else seriously for a while; instead she could find ease in the arms of whom ever she chose to be with for the moment. Chelae had at last come to accept that she didn't hate men because of her past, she simply loved women. Should it come to the point that true love knocked, she could only hope that she'd be brave enough to answer.

She wiggled into her dress and shook her hair. Soft curls bounced around her face as she headed to the bathroom to put on her make-up. When she saw a watery blur of herself she gasped. Quickly she reached for a towel. She wet the ends with cold water and began to pat around her puffy eyes. Chelae knew she cared about David a little, but she had to learn how to protect her own heart.

When she exited the bathroom the scent of Adonis's cologne still lingered quietly in the air. The smell of him caused her to inhale deeply and smile while thoughtful about his dimpled face and soft looking-lips. Her own cheeks became warm as she became anxious to get on with the day. His convinced demeanor and delicious smell of him was enough to look forward to, as it were.

Chelae's cheeks puffed out as she let the air gush past her lips. She walked over to the mirrored closet door. Chelae lifted her arms above her head for a visual inspection of her body. She'd been in New York less than a day, and life looked better for her. Chelae was pleased with her appearance and position as she smiled once more.

Chapter Eight - How you do that there?

Chelae made her way over to the nightstand to get her cell phone. She picked it up and went over to the window. Chelae had finally resolved to call her two girlfriends. She hated to have to explain her impromptu departure. It was time to call them and let them know she was in New York. She called Cora first.

"Hey girl, what's good? You were supposed to call me this morning. Tell David to stay off it long enough for you to make a phone call, damn." Cora said.

"I'm not with him. I left him last night."

"Really? Good, I couldn't stand his ass. Do you need help sitting his belongings on the curb? I have some boxes in the basement; I can bring them right over. Did you finally catch him with Lyn? "

"No. What do you mean caught him with Lyn?"

"Oh, I saw them last night at the hotel here on Eight Mile sitting in her truck. He was sucking her tits in public. They kissed and then he jumped out and caught a bus. Can you believe she wouldn't even give him a ride? My goodness she looks as old as my grandmother too. I can see why he did it thought. The one time I talked to her at a party she went on and on about how she basically pays for it. I mean really, I buy his clothes, shoes, pay his bills, whatever to keep mines happy. I thought how cheesy and hamburger hoe-like to myself, but I let her rant and talk about how good she thought she was. She looks like she could use a bath, a few tidal wave douches, and some microderm abrasion on that face. I could carry groceries in those bags under her eyes. She has a musty scent that seemed like it was stuck in her skin. I swear I wanted to push her down and wash her face myself. She's living with a man anyway. He works for the State and she's screwing out of both drawer legs. I've never liked her fake ass."

"Is that the first time you've seen them together?"

"No. I've done my best to get you to come and visit but you never do. I figured you were smart enough to catch them eventually. I didn't know how you would take it from me. Where are you, I'm on my way."

"I'm in New York right now."

"What? Why didn't you call me?"

"I'm sorry but I don't feel like hashing through the details right now. I need to call you back."

Chelae pushed the end call on her cell phone and began to pace the floor. She hadn't known about Lyn. She stopped and leaned her back against the chilly glass window pane. The coolness calmed her.

She looked down at the phone in her hand and with a frustrated grunt threw it against the hotel wall. It came apart, but it wasn't broken. It finally made sense why Lyn had been so friendly towards her. She'd stomached her, but she'd never really cared for her.

Chelae then called Lesley as well but it went to voicemail. She felt herself slide down towards the floor. Chelae willed her knees not to buckle completely and forced herself to stand back up straight. She ran her hands through her hair and walked over to the nightstand. Her fingers clutched the cradle of the phone as she dialed David's cell phone.

"Hello" he said.

"Where are you?"

"I'm at the mall.

"In them all, I bet you were. "

"Where are you?"

"None of your business. I'll be back to Detroit soon enough."

"I miss you and I'm sorry. I shouldn't say it like that."

"Later"

She'd hung up the phone. Chelae felt her nerves beginning to falter. The shock stung when she tried to put it together in her head. She reached up with her free hand to her forehead and pressed her temple. Her other hand lingered on the cradle of the phone a while.

Chelae bent down to recover the pieces of her cell phone from the floor to put it back together. She walked slowly over to the bed with the parts in her hand. Her cheeks rounded as she sucked in a deep breath when she sat down on the edge the bed. Nervously, she chewed her bottom lip.

She realized that Lyn had been after David from the first day she spoken to them. She'd seen Lyn at plenty of functions, but she'd never spoken to with her other than dry grunt of acknowledgment. Then they'd run across her at his cousin Murphy's birthday party, at the Marriot, just a few weeks before, Lyn had followed them nearly all night.

Lyn asked her questions about their relationship status. David seemed to be pleasant enough towards her. Finally, Chelae had grown tired of the interview-like questions from Lyn and cut her off, in the middle of a sentence.

"It's been a pleasure talking to you." Chelae said.

She abruptly walked away headed towards the balcony. As she quickly stepped through the balcony doors, she felt Lyn stare at her. In her haste, she nearly slipped. She felt a sure, strong hand in the small of her back. She turned and found herself in the face of Kristen.

"I thought that was you earlier, you almost took a dive. How have you been?"

"I've been managing, thank you. How have you been?"

"Things have been as okay as they can be. Are you here with someone or…?"

"I am on a date tonight. You?"

"No. You know me better than that."

"I've always wished that I did."

"You tell me when it's too late. That's when I'll quit waiting for my second chance."

Chapter Nine - Real as it Gets

Adonis was very concerned with his career and how he appeared to others. He was a bald, five foot eleven, wide framed man. He dressed sharply most of the time. He kept a strict limit on his diet because of his bouts with hypertension. One of the side effects from his life-saving medication was erectile dysfunction.

His marriage to Rayon was arranged. He was disappointed when he'd found his wife had a ravenous sexual appetite for anything human, except him. He was deceptive about his talents and skills, an expert at cover-ups, but looked like a real gem to those around him.

His self-esteem was tied up in how he appeared to people he liked. The fear of failure was unbearable, especially since his first marriage had fallen apart. He'd met with some success, but the drive to be better overtook him.

He took undue credit at the expense of the team. Still, Adonis knew he was phony. He was prone to moods swings that were filled with self-doubt. He'd successfully pulled off his facade, but sensed that it could crumble at any moment.

Adonis was on the edge of a nervous break-down since he discovered his wife; Rayon had cheated on him with other men and women. He'd changed career goals after he'd screwed a business partner and his wife out of money. The husband had shown up every day for nearly two years to help to build a Flower shop business. He'd driven his vehicle for deliveries, stayed late and put up with some of the craziest demands from customers.

In the end he'd grown tired of the excuses and left. Shortly afterward it had become difficult to find employment. He'd never really known why until he'd run across a mutual associate. He told him he was at a meeting when his name had come up as a Candidate for a position as Lead supervisor of the Marketing Department.

He explained to him that the only person who'd objected had been his former partner. He didn't believe it at first but he'd begin to notice that whenever his applications went through somewhere that he'd been. It never panned out.

Finally one day, his former partner called and him asked him to verify his employment for a new job. He'd known about how he'd tried to play him yet he helped. Adonis decided that it wasn't going to help to hold him back. His former business partner didn't realize not only did he not need the job, he was independently wealthy. Adonis was owner of The Seasons Hotel.

Self-esteem had become a real issue for him. Adonis was able to compromise himself to gain his wife's affection at the start. However, a sense of entitlement caused him to become manipulative at times to get the sympathy from her. He wanted to be recognized as indispensable, even if it meant another woman. He'd invited Chelae to lunch to make him feel better about his wife's deceitfulness.

Although Chelae and Adonis had only shared a meal, he had hoped that his wife found out from the hotel staff and became jealous. It was an example of his tendency to manipulate others. He'd led Chelae to believe he was single, but the fact was, he'd never told her he was married.

His wife was a personal slice of hell. Rayon was selfish and heartless. She was a forceful person obsessed with control. She had the desire to lead a great power, but hidden inner insecurities had made it possible only to lead those weak enough to be easily dominated.

Rayon was a thick, dark brown complexioned woman. She wore wigs to cover her heavily grayed hair. She had a large mole on her cheek. She dressed much younger than her fifty three years old. Rayon often wore skin-tight clothes that showed every nook and cranny.

Rayon had enrolled in a Turbo Thighs program to lose weight. She stood at five foot four, but weighed a hefty two hundred and fifty eight pounds.

She had pushed insecurity aside so she could focus on control. Rayon believed that if she could control a lot of people or a system, then she wasn't really insecure and she could overcome her fear as irrational. She'd always hung out with other people much younger than her. There she'd found a level of acceptance from a crowd immature enough to respect her and childish enough to support her whims.

Rayon didn't care about people and would to do whatever it took to increase her control. She was attracted to weak followers with issues of their own. She gave little thought about whether to betray or destroy them to prove her ability to control. Meanwhile, she'd been known to fuck whatever moved.

She'd thought of herself as discreet, but the men she'd screwed wasted little time to brag about it and word had already made its way back to her husband. He loved her and had become defensive whenever other's tried to warn him about her "boyfriends".

The men where she worked as a Medical Clerk would only talk to her briefly. Most of them knew about her ways either through rumors or firsthand. She'd had one friend, Sandy. Sandy didn't think of her as a friend though, she'd seen her as a mere business acquaintance.

As a hospital employee, Rayon was privileged to corner what many long for. She gained the ability to communicate with doctors daily. Unfortunately, she'd spent a good deal of it to use her mouth for activities not related to patient care. When her husband heard the rumors, he was hurt. Rayon noticed a change in Adonis's behavior, but hadn't inquired about it.

Adonis hadn't been entirely honest with Rayon either. When he married her, he'd lead her to believe that he had worked many years in Hotel Hospitality. He'd told her that he started as a porter and worked his way up to

Front Desk Clerk at various Hotels and Resorts around Albany. Rayon hadn't questioned his description of his past.

He'd just purchased a house for them, so she didn't have to travel so far to work. When he asked her to ride with him, she sighed but went along. Rayon spent the entire time on her cell phone as he drove. He'd already gotten out of the car and opened the door before she'd paid any attention.

Rayon leaped from the car with a childish squeal and raced inside the house, through a glass patio door into a spacious kitchen. She laid her cell phone on the counter and quickly darted from room to room. Adonis grinned as she twirled around in the large foyer with her arm stretched out wide. Rayon smiled brightly.

Adonis waited in the kitchen until she'd returned out of breath and excited. He pulled her close to him, circled his arms around her waist and kissed her. His cell phone began to vibrate in his front pocket and he'd taken it out, laid it on the counter and continued to kiss his wife.

He was glad she was happy. She'd already begin to talk excitedly about how to decorate the place. Adonis told her that he'd had a run to make. He promised to return quickly, as he picked up the phone from the counter. He'd planned to go to Home Depot to buy new locks and temporary shades.

Rayon had gotten what she wanted, more gifts. She'd grown up in a poor area of Belize. She'd come to America as an adopted fourth grader. Since her arrival, she been gracious and pleased when she received things that she saw as a privilege.

She wanted to call Sandy and boast about her gift. She'd watched through a bay window as her husband pulled from the curb, then she beamed at her good fortune. She made her way back to the kitchen to grab her phone. Rayon gasped when she noticed that phone on the counter wasn't hers.

Adonis had easily found a parking spot when the cell phone rang. He continued to park, while he reached for the phone. He'd pushed the green button when he put the phone to his ear.

"Shit, I can't even drive right now. Still, thinking about those big juicy lips sucking my dick. Meet me in the basement, so I can pull those panties to the side and bust in that hot ass. I love the way those hips was moving when you was bent over the washing machine." Terrell said.

"Huh?"

"Don't play with me Ray, I saw you walking away ever so slowly. I had to shoot a move or I would have stayed with you a little longer. Call me when that punk ass man of yours goes to work. I'll come over and put a pounding on that ass."

Adonis hung up the phone. He put his hands on the steering wheel and gripped it tightly. His knuckles began to turn white. His chest heaved and felt as though it would cave in, while he'd fought the urge not to cry. The way the man had spoken told him more than he'd ever wanted to know.

It took all of his courage not call the man and question him. Adonis had suspected that she'd had secrets. Another man wasn't in his thoughts. Although he'd had no problem to confront him about his wife. Adonis didn't feel this was an issue to confront the guy about. He was angry with her. He couldn't shake the thought that she'd sucked another mans' dick but kissed him on the lips.

He opened the car door and swung his legs onto the concrete. The vomit had already made its way into his mouth. Adonis leaned and opened his lips and heaved while everything he'd consumed rolled out. When he was done, he laid his head in his hands and began to cry in the Home Depot Parking Lot.

He'd sat in the car for a full thirty minutes. It'd taken him that long to even get his thoughts to stop the echo of what he'd heard. In the same length of time, he'd envisioned some random stranger on his wife in some of the most sordid positions. Determined to pull himself together, he'd started the car and left to go find fresh water and something for pain. His head banged.

Adonis drove to a gas station nearby and ran in to get medicine for his headache. He settled on a pack of Advil, some apple juice and bottled water. When he'd paid for his items, he went behind the building to rinse his mouth out with the water. He gulped large swigs of the cold fluid and swished it around. The water seemed to renew the taste of acid and he gagged as he spat it on the ground. After he'd gotten himself together, Adonis decided that he would go back, give her the phone and keep quiet.

He drove to their new house slowly. Adonis dreaded to see her face. He wondered if she'd be able to tell that he knew. It was time for her to make a seminar that she'd told him she had scheduled that morning over breakfast. As he pulled up in front of the house, Adonis did his best to act normal.

He'd barely put the car in park, when Rayon ran out of the house. Adonis told her the lines were too long and that he'd change the locks later. Rayon pleaded with him to take her back to her car, so she could make it to her seminar on time. She'd assured him she would come back promptly afterwards to celebrate with him and then winked at her husband flirtatiously.

After they'd secured the house, he drove her back home. As Rayon jumped from the car, she'd raced over to kiss him. Adonis did his best not to recoil as she puckered her lips. He quickly pecked her lips and she was off.

Adonis had given her a few minutes to get a head start, and then pulled out into traffic. He'd followed as she drove erratically down the Albany streets until she reached the I-90 highway entrance. Rayon merged into the flow of traffic and sped towards her destination. Adonis positioned himself in the slow lane so that he'd be able to see where she'd exit.

Twenty minutes later, the flow of traffic slowed and he saw his wife merge onto the I-87 toll road. Adonis had begun to feel silly for trailing her and was tempted to turn around. His heart wouldn't let him return without an answer. The sun shone brightly and he'd been able to hide most of his face behind his visor.

After he'd paid his toll, he spotted Rayon's car as it swerved around a bend that headed around a mountain. Adonis continued to follow until he saw his wife's car pull off the road into a truck rest. Several trucks lined the massive lot. Adonis had lost sight of her vehicle and drove around to the back of the small building that housed washrooms.

A large grey awning stood in the rear of the building. He spotted her vehicle at last. Adonis pulled up a few spots away from Rayon's car. It was empty.

The sun had begun to set as Adonis made his way under the structure on foot. It'd taken less than a minute to figure out which car she'd gotten into. The fresh mountain air and deep cleft in the mountains of Catskills, NY had provided a serene hush compared to the noise of Albany. He'd heard her shrill laughter come from his left. He ducked down in between the rows to get closer. The shiny silver Jaguar was parked in the opposite direction and far away from the other vehicles.

Adonis inched closer and could overhear their conversation.

"Oh fuck, I'm so hungry I could swallow you whole right now." Rayon said.

"That's what I like about you. You don't hold a nigga up with the bullshit. You ain't got no shame in licking my dick anywhere. I thought you weren't coming to see me."

"Why? When you call me and talk that shit to me, you get me so wet. You're so different from my husband. Not afraid to say what you want."

"What the fuck did I tell you about mentioning that him to me? That shit right there makes my jimmy soft. I don't want to think about another man. He doesn't know me and I don't know him. I'm trying to fuck with you. Get your thick ass over here and suck me up."

Adonis was tempted to walk over to the car and slap the shit out of him. The thought that she'd cringed every he tried to touch her in the past was made him angrier. He'd never spoken to her that way or asked her to do anything like that. Adonis clenched his fist as he watched her leaned over towards the man in driver's seat.

Rayon's head disappeared into the man's lap. Adonis started to walk back to his own car. He'd seen enough, although he hadn't seen the face of Rayon's lover. Adonis walked back to his car and got and left. He was livid.

Chapter Ten - Keep in Touch

Chelae felt the strong urge to grab her "playthings" from her bag and take care of the problem that Adonis had created. It was unusual for her to be turned on by a man. Her creative imagination could allow her to have her way with him freely courtesy of her toy.

He'd never be the wiser and she'd be less stressed. Just the same, Chelae decided against it and jumped back into the shower instead. At least this way the fresh moisture would be washed away before she was dressed, she reasoned.

Nearly two hours later, Chelae was dressed and called down to the front desk. Several rings later a sultry male voice greeted her. Immediately Chelae's mind was invaded with a picture of a naked Adonis, fully hard and a tad sweaty. Chelae gulped before she spoke.

"Hi, this is Ms. Thomas in room 313, I was about to come down. Is Adonis available?" Chelae said.

"This is Adonis. I'm definitely ready for you." He said.

"I'll be there shortly."

Chelae picked up her purse and took one more look at her in the long mirror on the wall. The short floral print dress clung to the flair of her hips. She'd chosen to wear a black jacket that was cut at her waist with a scalloped collar that accentuated her breasts. The crisp sunrise air had helped her decide on black satin knee-hi boots with a four-inch spike heel. Chelae felt her outfit brought that famous Detroit class to her New York trip.

She checked her lips once more and pinched her cheeks again for a natural blush effect before she left. Her mind had already begun to wander as she pushed the button and waited on the elevator. It felt like an eternity to her as she caught herself when she'd held her breath while the seconds ticked by, until the elevator finally opened. Chelae had taken the opportunity to check her teeth in the shiny silver slabs.

When the door opened for her to enter the box, she gasped. The young porter who helped them to their rooms the day before was inside the car. Two suitcases lay overturned on the floor. A woman who appeared to be in her early fifties had him pressed into the corner. He looked over her the woman's shoulder at Chelae. Just then Chelae noticed that the woman furiously brushed against his groin area through his pants. His eyes pleaded with Chelae to interrupt.

Chelae reached inside the car and hit the button to close the door. She didn't get in the elevator. The grimace on the porter's faces said "I hate you" as Chelae watched the doors close again. She brushed off her shoulder and waited for the next elevator instead.

When the car returned a few moments later it was empty. Chelae giggled as she stepped inside and wondered what had happened to the young man and his eager cougar guest. When the car reached the lobby, the doors opened and she found Adonis there. He checked his watch.

"You didn't have to meet me at the elevator." Chelae said.

"I just happened to be passing when I saw it was coming down. Shall we?" Adonis said.

He extended his arm towards Chelae as if expected her to link hers into his. Chelae raised her eyebrow and shook her head no. Adonis shrugged his shoulders and swept his hand in front of him. Chelae smirked as she left the elevator and walked in front of Adonis.

The tiny stringed thong gave no support to her ass cheeks under the snug dress. Chelae could feel the heat rays from Adonis's eyes as she walked. Adonis felt his dick grow in his pants as he watched her hips sway. He wondered if she was aware that he could nearly see the plump folds of her bottom through her dress.

When they reached the doorway of the first conference room, Chelae ventured inside. Adonis walked up beside her and cleared his throat before he explained the sizes of the rooms could be adjusted by the square foot. The walls were really extra-large cubicle dividers that were moved easily. Armed with that information in mind, Chelae decided that the room itself was suitable.

"Okay, that's cool." Chelae said.

"Ready to grab a bite to eat?" Adonis asked.

"Actually, a cup of coffee and something light sounds wonderful."

"Then follow me."

Adonis took the lead and began to escort Chelae to George's Bistrouille, which was inside the lobby of the hotel. She waited while Adonis signaled for the attention of the hostess. When the plump matronly woman came over, Adonis leaned over and whispered in her ear. The woman smiled brightly and waved for them to follow her.

After they arrived at the table, the hostess introduced herself to Chelae.

"Hi, I'm Beatrice and welcome to George's. Can I get you something to drink to start out with?" She said.

Chelae asked for a coffee and Adonis stayed quiet. The woman walked away and hummed. Chelae raised her eyebrow in confusion as she realized that Adonis hadn't ordered. He placed a menu from a silver stand in the middle of the table and passed one to Chelae before he looked up into her face. Sensing Chelae's confusion he spoke up.

"Beatrice knows exactly what I want." Adonis said.

"Oh" Chelae said.

She remained quiet as she read the menu. The description of the Pecan Crusted Chicken Salad made her mouth water. When Beatrice returned to the table with the coffee and a Glass of Merlot, she smiled as she placed them on the table.

"What are you having?" She asked Chelae.

"The Pecan Chicken Salad sounds scrumptious. Do you have a light dressing though? Like Strawberry Vinaigrette?" Chelae inquired.

"Let me see what I can do. George makes his famous house dressing fresh every day. I swear that man loves to cook though. I'm sure he can whip up a batch just for you, although he can be as stubborn as a mule sometimes, he's in a pretty good mood right now." Beatrice said.

Beatrice left the table to put in their order. A few moments later, Chelae heard shouts come from the kitchen. Adonis put his hand over his mouth to hide his laughter. Chelae leaned over to look past Adonis and see what had caused the commotion.

"Just make the damn dressing. Ain't nothing to argue about, I said gets to making it, now get it done."

"Damn woman, always coming in here trying to tell me what to do. You just wait 'til somebody comes here order the Pork Chops. I'm a get you for this; don't be coming in here making more work for me. Ain't shit wrong with the house dressing." George yelled.

"Shut up."

Chelae sat back upright. She looked at Adonis. He snorted and flailed his arms with laughter. She shook her head and laughed as well. Beatrice and George definitely had a sense of humor that Adonis found hilarious. Chelae quickly realized that Adonis was used to their shenanigans. After their laughter subdued, Adonis turned his attention back to Chelae.

"So what kind of business brings you New York?" Adonis asked.

"How about you tell me something about you instead?" Chelae replied.

"What do you want to know?"

"Where do you shop at? I mean you seem to be very stylish. I was just wondering if perhaps you were into fashion or just happened to have an eye for tasteful clothing."

"I don't know about having an eye for fashion, but I do have an eye for beautiful women."

"I'm innocent of that accusation."

"Oh no, you are guilty as sin."

"Are you flirting with me?"

"Is it working?"

"I don't think that's the best course of action, seeing as how I'm leaving in a few days. What could possibly become of this?

Chapter Eleven - Heart Strings

When Kristen woke up, she stretched and yawned then wiggled her toes. The trip was a much needed get-away for her. She'd wanted to talk to Chelae, but Chelae had always been busy.

The more Kristen thought about it, the more she was glad that Chelae had called on her to come with. She secretly hoped that it meant more than just what Chelae had said. It angered when Chelae had called her in tears over some guy. After all they'd faced together, Kristen still loved Chelae deeply.

Kristen had often wished that Chelae could wipe away the pain she had caused her in the past. However, Chelae had a way to make her suffer for it. Even though Chelae didn't flaunt other lovers in front of Kristen, she said just enough to piss Kristen off. Chelae had assumed that the thought of anyone between her thighs was like a nightmare while she was awake for Kristen.

Kristen had always wanted to be the center of Chelae's heart. What Chelae had given her was affection and incredible escapades of kinky sexual adventure. Still it was the impression that Chelae had the ability to be steamy hot or icy cold that frightened Kristen when it came to giving her all.

The first action Kristen took, after she'd sat upright in the luxurious bed, was reach for the phone to call Chelae's room. She looked at the phone directory card laid it on the nightstand and found Chelae's room number. The phone rang several times. Chelae didn't answer and Kristen huffed with frustration.

She decided to shower and try again afterwards. A half-hour later, Kristen was fully dressed as she stood in the mirror brushed her freshly cut waves in place. Satisfied that she was appropriately groomed, she sauntered to the stand and tried Chelae once more.

She tried Chelae's cell phone as well. Chelae answered on the third ring.

"Hey, you're woke." Chelae said.

"Yeah, you ready to go grab a bite to eat?" Kristen asked.

"Actually, I just ate. Would you like me to bring you something up?"

Adonis had begun speak to some of the other hotel guests as they wandered into George's. Kristen overheard him in the background. Chelae held the phone and waited on a response from her. The phone hung up abruptly and Chelae sighed.

Chelae did her best to smile in spite of it while she thanked Adonis for the meal and excused herself. He stood up and followed her to the Bistro door. Chelae reached in her purse and gave Adonis a business card to keep in touch. Adonis took the card and gripped it so hard that it crumpled it his hand.

Chelae had barely made it into the main portion of the lobby when she paused. Her heart began to pound wildly in her chest. The large open space suddenly seemed as small as an airplane bathroom to her. She blinked several times. Chelae refused to believe her eyes.

Thess was at the hotel counter check- in. Before Chelae could gain her composure, Thess turned and look directly at her and smiled. Chelae took small steps towards Thess. Thess turned and began to walk towards Chelae. She'd closed the gap between them in a matter of seconds.

Chelae shuddered inside as Thess wrapped her arms around her waist and hugged her tightly. The scent of her cologne created a scrumptious cloud of seduction. Chelae was unable to move. Thess leaned back slightly and looked in Chelae's eyes.

"What are you doing here Thess?" Chelae asked.

"Aren't you glad to see me baby?" Thess said.

"You didn't answer my question."

"You didn't answer me either."

Chelae gently placed her hand on Thess's chest to push away from her. Thess gripped her waist firmly, rebuffed the idea to break the embrace. Chelae was about to demand that Thess release her immediately. Just then, the elevator door opened and Kristen stepped out.

"Thess please let me go." Chelae said.

"No. I came all the way here to see you. I thought you'd be happy to see me." Thess said.

"Look bitch, you have one second to get your hands off of my wife like she asked you or I will spread your ass all over this lobby like cheap peanut butter." Kristen said.

Thess let go and turned to face Kristen. The two glared at each other for a full minute. Kristen reached around Thess and grabbed Chelae's hand and pulled her closer. Chelae nearly fell from the unexpected movement of her body.

"Chelae, what the hell is she doing here?" Thess asked.

"Me? I came with her. The question is what the fuck are you doing here?" Kristen asked.

Chelae put her hand up between the two women. Thess stepped forward aggressively. Kristen balled her fists up and Chelae realized that she was prepared to swing. She moved her body between the two women to prevent the fight. She'd hoped that neither woman would hit her.

"Chelae, I haven't disrespected you but honestly if you're still seeing her then you're trifling. You lied to me and told me it was over between you two." Thess shouted.

"First of all Thess, I didn't lie but that's not your business. I invited Kristen. When I spoke to you last, you had met someone. Why are you here?" Chelae asked again.

"Who gives a damn? She came, she saw, and I hope she was just leaving." Kristen said.

"That's not going to happen Kristen. I just checked in. I'll be here for a few days. And to answer your question Chelae, I came to get my woman." Thess said.

"Where is she at?" Kristen asked.

"I'm not talking to you, I'm talking to Chelae." Thess said.

"Man you still ain't learned shit. You find a fool and bump their head. She didn't leave me the first time for you and she's not leaving now. The way you be chasing my woman is sad." Kristen said.

Adonis heard the heated exchange and rushed over with Beatrice in tow. Chelae tugged at Kristen's hand. Thess began to speak to Adonis and Beatrice explaining the situation. Kristen eventually followed Chelae to the elevators.

Kristen and Chelae were about to get in when Thess shouted across the lobby.

"I won't rest until she's mine Kristen." Thess said.

"Well, you're going to be a sleepy bitch then." Kristen replied.

Kristen and Chelae had scarcely made it inside of the elevator car, when Kristen turned on her.

"So you left me in the room so that you could go eat with her? Don't lie either, I saw y'all hugging and you were about to kiss her too. You could have left me at home. I can't believe that you brought me all this way to hoe around with her." Kristen said.

"But, I didn't. I was about to…" Chelae said.

Kristen threw her hand up in Chelae's face and cut her off.

"The two of you are not going to take me through this shit again. I'm not playing with you. Bay, do you hear me? I'm serious. You are not to ever see her again." Kristen said.

"Wait a minute. That's funky as hell considering all the stuff you've done and she's not a bitch." Chelae said.

"You see any other woman wearing shit I paid for? Do you see any hoes showing up when I'm with you? No, okay then respect me like I respect you. Keep that bullshit in check." Kristen said.

"I didn't know though." Chelae said.

Chelae crossed her arms and fought back tears. Kristen looked at her and saw her bottom lip poked out and quivered. Kristen began to feel bad for the way she'd snapped at Chelae. She reached over and clutched Chelae's hand before she tenderly wiped away the tears from her plump cheek.

"Bay stop, you messing up your make-up and you're gonna be pissed when your face is all puffy. I'm not hunting through the streets of New York to find no damn cucumber slices for your eyes. There's nothing about her worth you crying for." Kristen said.

"You told her I was your wife. Why?" Chelae sniffed.

Kristen just looked at Chelae and shook her head.

Chapter Twelve - Knew Porter

Adonis had left the counter thirty minutes before his get-together with Chelae. When he'd finally calmed Thess down and escorted her to room, he returned to man the front desk. The porter appeared from nowhere and asked if there was anything he could do. The young man had just started at the hotel a few weeks before and Adonis was impressed with his hard working.

"Terrell, I noticed that you work really hard around here. I just wanted to say I noticed and I'm keeping my eye on you. You have a bright future around here if you keep that up." Adonis said.

"Thank you, I'll keep that in mind." Terrell replied.

The porter turned and saw a cab pull into the hotel driveway. He went over the door and held it open for the elderly couple that approached the lobby doors. Terrell led them to the front desk for Adonis to check them in, while he helped the driver get their luggage.

"Hello Mrs. Olivia, so nice to see you back." Adonis said.

"Good to see you too dear." Mrs. Olivia replied.

Terrell raced past them to get the cart. It seemed Mrs. Olivia had brought enough luggage to stay for the entire season. Once he'd finally had the luggage on the cart and caught up with the couple, they were already at the elevator. He was winded and out of breath as he pushed the now loaded cart towards the elevator bay.

"You two go ahead and I'll be up in a minute." Terrell said.

Mrs. Olivia nodded in agreement and stepped inside the car. Mr. Olivia rarely spoke. He held the door for his wife to get inside the car and picked-up her Tunichi fur to keep the door from closing on it. She smiled as she pulled her gloves off and stuck them in her purse.

Five minutes later, Terrell arrived at the Olivia's door and knocked. Mrs. Olivia opened it.

After he unloaded the cart, Mr. Olivia passed him a crisp fifty dollar bill and held the door for him to leave with the cart. Mrs. Olivia waited until Terrell was out of the room and cleared her throat to get his attention. After he'd pushed the cart out of the door, Terrell turned to tell them to enjoy their stay.

"Excuse me, but it seems you have a bit of lipstick on your shirt collar." Mrs. Olivia said.

"Oh, thank you." He said.

"Yeah, it's some on your pants too, you might want to change." Mr. Olivia said.

Terrell felt his face get warm and quickly began to push the cart up the hall. Just as the Olivia's closed their hotel door, Rayon opened the door and stepped out into the hall. Terrell nearly ran into her with the cart. She pushed past the cart and walked up to Terrell and gripped his firm ass. He yelped and gripped the cart frame, before he'd swung his head back and forth to see if anyone saw what she'd done.

"Aw, come on. I just started this gig. Don't get me fired please. It's bad enough that you've stalked me to my new job. I can't have you showing up here. What if someone finds out? Go home and I'll call you in a while, but please don't show back up here Ray. "Terrell begged.

"I won't make any trouble for you. I'll stay a while. You will come see me again later, yes?" Rayon asked.

"I'm off in a couple of hours; I don't think that's possible. I did enjoy you though. I'll call you later."

"You come back in a few minutes then."

"No. You're trying my patience woman. What did you do? Follow me to work, where's your husband? Look, I don't want to hurt your feelings but this isn't going to work. I ain't up for a chick that will chase me down for the pole. Alright, now go home."

He'd hardly made it into the elevator when Rayon went back inside her room. She'd occupied the room next to the Olivia's. She was about to pick the phone up and call the front desk and request the Bell Boy to her room, when she heard a woman scream. Terrell was already on his way back to the lobby.

Curiously, Rayon went onto the balcony. The occupants in the room next to hers had left their balcony doors open and she could hear them clearly. She eased closer to the edge closest to their room and listened. Rayon could overhear the woman as if she was in the room with them.

"You fucking simpleton. You met that woman over at the Café' and you are going to pay dearly for it." Mrs. Olivia screamed.

"But I..." Mr. Olivia said.

"Shut the fuck up. You want a bitch to spank you. You fucking pervert. You have exactly three seconds to take those damn clothes off. Lay your ass across the bed."

"Honey, I…"

"Say one more word and I will drag your ass through the messiest fucking divorce you have ever seen. I promise you I will use every bit of influence that I have to make your life a living hell."

"Okay, okay."

"Okay my ass."

"I did it, now what are you going to do me."

Rayon flinched when she heard the loud slap. Mr. Olivia yapped and then grunted. Several more hits rained down in rapid succession. Rayon giggled when the man at last cried out pleading with his wife to stop.

"Now I'm going to piss and when I come back guess what I'm using for tissue? Your tongue, that's what. I can't believe you spent a dollar on a common street walker. I've been married to you too long for you to be giving a penny to a whore. It never crossed your mind to tell me what you wanted huh? I bet you'll be more forthcoming after tonight, won't you?"

"Yes ma'am."

She'd heard enough and Rayon went back inside her own room. She felt the heat grow between her thighs. As kinky as it was it still served to stir her sexual appetite.

She decided to wait another hour before she called the front desk and summon the porter. Instead she could entertain herself and eavesdrop on her twisted temporary neighbors. Rayon eased back on the balcony again just in time to hear Mrs. Olivia bark orders.

"Get over here and clean me. That's all you're good for is a filthy little ass rag." Mrs. Olivia said.

"Yes." He said.

A few minutes passed before finally Rayon heard the woman moan. The sound of the woman as she had such an intense orgasm caused Rayon to inhale sharply. A prickle of envy ran through her body. She was certain that she would call the front desk and have the porter sent up right away.

Rayon rifled through her purse and found a scarf. Adrenaline coursed through her veins, as she dialed the front desk. When Adonis answered, she placed the scarf over the phone and spoke with a fake foreign accent. Adonis agreed readily to send the porter up to her room.

"Terrell, there is a guest in room 215 that needs your assistance." Adonis said.

When Terrell heard the room number he grimaced. He'd already regretted the old cougar as it were. There was no way he was about to go back into the room with her, if he could avoid it. Terrell had no idea that Rayon would continue to call for him. She'd just shown up expectantly at his job. Terrell had checked her in while Adonis was at lunch.

"Look Adonis, she wants more than a little room service. I see you're a married man. You have a better chance of getting her to step off than I would okay. I will gladly hold down the front desk for you but if you don't mind can you go up instead, just this once?" Terrell pleaded.

"Okay, it's not like we haven't had a lonely guest or two before. I'll handle her. Don't worry though, you will get used to it. Is that how you got that make-up on your shirt?" Adonis asked.

Terrell nodded yes.

"Well I hate to be the one to tell you, but you have some on your zipper too. Had enough?" Adonis joked.

Terrell blushed and turned his head away. Adonis left him alone and headed towards the elevator to the second floor. He had planned to explain to the woman in no uncertain terms that he wasn't interested, if she hit on him. He'd done it before and he was pretty comfortable with being able to reject any advances, should it come to that."

"Man, I'm warning you. She is fine as hell. Her booty just makes you stop and stare. Be careful. I don't know her like that but I'm telling you, undercover freak is an understatement."

Chapter Thirteen - Always

Chelae went her room with an angry Kristen in tow. Kristen took the keys from Chelae's hand and opened the hotel room door. Chelae went into the room and flopped across the bed. Kristen went into the bathroom and started Chelae a warm bath.

While the water filled the tub, Kristen returned to the bed and unbuttoned Chelae's jacket. She sat with her bottom lip still poked out as Kristen undressed her slowly and methodically. Chelae held her arms up as Kristen pulled her dress over her head.

Kristen stood back and took in the site of Chelae as she sat on the bed in a thong, bra and knee-hi boots. Kristen felt the moisture roll in between her own thighs as she took in the sight of Chelae's soft, buttery skin exposed. The fat mound between her thighs seemed to beckon Kristen to bury her face in that spot. Kristen chose to wait.

Chelae reluctantly lifted her legs as Kristen removed her boots. When Kristen grabbed her hand and pulled her to the bathroom, Chelae went along. Chelae looked Kristen in the eyes as she watched Kristen's hands wobble while she unsnapped her bra.

The cool air made Chelae nipples harden instantly. Kristen fought the urge to take one in her mouth. Kristen bent over and slowly rolled Chelae's thong down over her hips to her ankles. As she rose up, she'd paused at Chelae's pussy. The heated aroma summoned her tongue from between Kristen's lips.

Kristen knew that Chelae was emotionally exhausted. She waited until Chelae stepped from her panties and helped her into the tub. Her hands held Chelae's waist while she steadied herself in the slippery tub. Chelae slipped into the luxuriously warm water and heaved a sigh.

"Bay, thank you for this because I never thought you would understand. I know it looked bad when you walked up but…" Chelae said.

"Don't say nothing. Enjoy your bath. I'm going to run to my room and grab this fifth of Paul. I'll come back soon and make us a few drinks and then we can chill. The sun is going down and maybe by the time you're done, we can watch the sunset together or something. When I get back, I don't want to see no tears though. Okay?" Kristen said.

Chelae nodded yes and leaned back into the water and closed her eyes.

"Promise." Kristen asked.

"Yeah bay, I'm good." Chelae said.

"Good, I'll be back as soon as I can. Keep it tight alright. Don't give that to no body while I'm gone." Kristen joked.

"Who I'm gone give it to?" Chelae asked.

"Don't act like it's not a line of people trying to get my pie. I know I've made some mistakes. You have to know it wasn't about playing you bay. You just don't be around somebody that long and not have some type of feelings. I tried baby, just keep it tight alright?"

Chapter Fourteen - Melee'

Kristen made her way to her room. When the elevator opened on the second floor Kristen saw Adonis walk up the hall. She smiled at him and he smiled back. He walked over to Kristen and they shook hands.

"You okay now?" Adonis asked.

"Yeah, I apologize for that shit earlier man. I don't fuck with nobody, but I'm sick of that little motherfucker." Kristen said.

"I hear you. Just try to keep your cool if you can." Adonis said.

Adonis headed for room 215 and knocked on the door. Kristen had barely put her key in the door, when the door Adonis was at opened. Kristen went into her room and rummaged through her duffel bag and grabbed the liquor. She headed back out of the room just in time to hear Adonis snap out.

"Are you fucking serious? No, bitch I just bought you a house and you up in here sucking off the fucking help? You know what, I'm sick of your shit. That's it. I've had it with you. "Adonis screamed.

Kristen assumed that Adonis must have known the woman. She didn't scream for help as Adonis pushed his way into the room and slammed the door. Kristen wanted to get back to Chelae. She returned to the elevator.

Adonis voice boomed like thunder through the room. Mrs. Olivia had finally tired of her game with Mr. Olivia, who was sound asleep on the bed. She had gone to the balcony to have a cigarette and enjoy the air while she thought up his next punishment. Adonis's curses had made Mrs. Olivia pay attention as she sat up in the chair.

Inside the room Adonis had wrapped his massive hands around Rayon's throat. When he saw her struggle to breathe, he relented and eased up. Rayon went to reach for the phone. Adonis ripped the phone cord from the wall.

"I ought to wrapped this cord around your neck and strangle you with it." He growled.

Rayon shrank onto the bed. Adonis straightened his body and regained his composure. He looked around the room thoughtfully. Rayon's eyes nearly popped from the sockets. She'd never seen him so angry. Adonis smirked as he looked down at his wife and he unzipped his pants.

He reached down in one swift motion and started to shred her clothes from her body. Rayon was confused. She trembled but didn't fight back. Instead, she tried to reason with him.

"Baby, I'm sorry. It's not what it seems. I just needed to, umm… get the porter to umm… move some things around for me." Rayon said.

"For once shut the fuck up lying to me." Adonis said.

"I understand if you want a divorce."

"A divorce, did Terrell have some PCP on his dick when you sucked it? There's not going to be a divorce. Now take those fucking drawers off. "

"How did you know his name?"

"What did I just tell you to do?"

Rayon scurried out of her tattered clothes. Adonis gripped her upper arms and shoved her roughly on her stomach. The adrenaline had rushed to the tip off his dick in his anger. She hadn't seen that he was stiff as a board.

Adonis rubbed his index finger across Rayon's moist slit and ran it around her asshole. He took his hand and gripped the back of her head and pushed her face into the mattress. Rayon tensed as she felt the large mushroomed head spread her ass wide. He plunged between her thick cheeks.

"You're up too far Adonis. That's my butt. Let me do it." Rayon said.

"No, I'm right where I want to be. Put your hand in my way and I might break your arm. I got a few fantasies of my own to fulfill." Adonis replied.

Rayon squealed when he pushed his thick length up her ass. It felt as if someone had heaved a rigid piece of wood into her tiny slot to Rayon. She bit her bottom lip hard as her husband mercilessly sawed into her body. Adonis grimaced at the tightness of her plump and pliant ass.

She arched her back as Adonis fucked her. He felt his balls tighten and slowed his pace. Rayon slyly slid her hand near her pussy and fingered her clit. When Adonis resumed his speed, Rayon could feel him throbbing inside of her. He tightened his hand in her hair and boisterously he pumped thick cream deep into her bowels.

Adonis was spent as he rolled off his wife. Rayon slowly rose from the bed and gingerly stepped from the bed to the bathroom. She took a thick fluffy face towel from the hotel shelf. She turned on the faucet and wet it thoroughly with warm water.

Adonis raised his head from the mattress to see where Rayon had gone. When she tipped back into the room, he stiffened up. She took the warm rag and softly started to clean his semi-hard rod. When Rayon was done, she took him into her mouth and sensuously began to suck him deep into her throat.

"Oh damn Ray that feels so good. I hope I didn't hurt you."

Rayon let go of his tool with a loud slurp.

"No, just please don't ever hit me Adonis. I don't like to be hit, but that way you talked. I didn't think…"

"Rayon, I love you. You never mentioned that you liked that kind of talk. You didn't have to go to another someone else for that. Had you told me what you wanted, I would have done my best to give it to you. You could have taught me. Do you understand that? I'm your husband. You cheating on me made me feel like a punk."

"I was ashamed. How do you tell someone your secret desires and risk them thinking different of you? I love the way you treat me outside of the bed. Inside the bedroom, I'd like you to be more in control. I like being talked to. It doesn't have to be mean; it could be sexy, or encouraging. You get on me and hump as if I'm a rubber doll, then roll off and go to sleep. Every now and again I manage to get there with you but not very often. I wanted to ask you to talk to me, but I thought you'd think less of me. The truth is your words get me hot."

"Rayon wrapped those juicy lips around me and swallow me deep."

Rayon flicked her tongue out and wet the underside of his shaft before she sucked him into her throat. Adonis mumbled. Rayon reached up and grasped one of his massive hands and placed in the back of her head. Her husband cradled the back of her skull and worked her head up and down.

A few moments later, Adonis let his thoughts flow from his lips. He grew into a stiffness that he hadn't had since his early twenties. As his sac tightened Adonis felt the tickle in shaft. He pulled himself from Rayon's lips.

Adonis beckoned for Rayon to straddle him. Once she managed to get into position, Adonis speared his way into her dripping wet pussy. Her pulled her forward and took one of her swaying nipples into his mouth. Rayon moaned.

Adonis took his hands and placed them on her ass. Slowly, he fucked her. Rayon leaned onto his chest. Adonis pushed up into her with a firm plunge.

"Yeah baby, just like that. Shit this pussy is so tight. Your walls are sucking me. This is my mine and I don't ever want you to give it to anyone do you understand me."Adonis asked.

Rayon groaned but didn't respond. Adonis huffed before he flipped Rayon on her back in one smooth motion. He reached down and hoisted her legs up to her ears. Adonis banged into with furious long-stroked pace until Rayon cried out.

"I said that is my pussy. I want this on my dick everyday and only mine. Do you fucking understand?" Adonis asked.

"Yes" Rayon said.

"Look at me. You gone learn today. Push them big titties together. I want to see you touch them."

"Yes" Rayon said as she did.

"Tell me Ray, is it good to you? I never knew you'd like this shit. What do I have to do to please you? I'm holding back from busting as it is. You are so sexy to me right now baby and you feel so good. I want to make you cum too, tell me what to do."

"What you did earlier."

Adonis stopped midstride. He looked down at his wife and spread her legs farther apart so he could see face clearly. Rayon cupped her breast and sucked her right nipple into her mouth. Adonis pulled out of her dewy cavern and placed the head of dick in her tight ass.

He was well lubricated from his journey into her slick pussy. He pushed and felt her tight anal muscles give. Adonis grunted as she gripped him like a glove. When Adonis took her clit in between his fingers and gently rolled back and forth while he pumped into her, Rayon bit down on her bottom lip and squealed as she squirted hot juice.

Adonis was stunned. The sudden gush of from her was new to him. He felt a surge of pride that he'd caused her to squirt. Adonis leaned into Rayon and stroked for all he was worth until he exploded inside of her.

Rayon reached up and grabbed the back of her husband's head. She kissed him. Adonis was thrilled when he felt her suck his tongue out of his mouth. He continued to stroke her and to his surprise he felt his wife's body shudder as waves of her orgasm overtook her in response.

"I do love you Adonis. I didn't know that it would be this good with you. I won't have another again, I promise." Rayon said.

Adonis collapsed into her soft bosom as soon as he slid out of her back door. His heart thumped in his chest. The blow to ego had from her cheating had been soothed. He'd felt partially to blame. Now that he'd found the key to his wife's secret door of desires, he'd planned to be the only person that she needed to come in.

\

Chapter Fifteen - Numbers is 313

When Kristen returned to Chelae's room, she found that she'd still rested peacefully in the tub. She heard the water run and knew that Chelae had re-heated her bath for the second time. Kristen cussed under her breath as she realized she hadn't brought anything to mix the Brandy with. Kristen went into the bathroom to inform Chelae that she was on her way to find a chaser for the drinks.

Chelae agreed and Kristen left. Patiently Kristen waited for the elevator once more. As she stepped out into the lobby, she saw Thess. Kristen's nostrils flared and she held her head up and walked past her as if Thess was invisible. Thess stared at Kristen but didn't speak.

Kristen found a vending machine and grabbed a few cans of Coke. She had decided that nothing would please her more than if Chelae would let her make her love to her tonight. It had been so long since she had touched her treasures. The more Kristen thought of Chelae's thighs wrapped around her, the quicker she stepped. She saw Thess as she'd sat alone at the bar and Kristen felt a little sorry for her. She remembered what Chelae was like in bed and as a person. Sadly, she understood the why Thess would go to any lengths to get with her. Unfortunately for Thess, Kristen wasn't about to let her go easily.

Finally, Kristen had made it back to the room and made the drinks. Just as she'd managed to sit Chelae's drink on the nightstand, Kristen looked up and saw her stand in the doorway. Chelae had oiled her body down and beads of water dripped from her body. Kristen took a big swig of her drink.

Chelae paced her as she walked to the bed and lay down. Kristen watched in silence. At last she felt Chelae move towards her and lay her head on Kristen's lap. Kristen reached down and stroked Chelae's hair. The heat from Chelae's breath warmed Kristen's thigh.

"How was your bath, Bay?" Kristen asked.

"It felt good but it was a little lonely."

"It's not like you invited me or anything."

"Really, I didn't know you needed an invitation."

Kristen sat her glass down and moved Chelae's head. Chelae propped up on her elbow and watched as Kristen went and cut off the bathroom light. When she came back and cut the bedroom light off, Chelae smirked. She could see Kristen's silhouette as she began undress. Chelae scurried up to the head of the bed and laid her head on the pillow.

Chelae's hotel room phone began to ring. She reached over and answered it. Kristen watched Chelae's body tense up as she held the phone to her ear. Chelae dropped her head.

"Come to my room and let me please you. I know you're only hesitating because of her. Chelae, I promise that if you will have me as your only woman, you will never spend a night wondering where I am or what I'm doing. I could see it in your eyes. Tell her the truth baby. Tell her it's me that you love and come and get your man.

We've been through too much for me to just let you go like this. I've given up everything to be with you. Take the chance on me, Chelae and do what you feel in your heart. You know we belong together and you know that it's me that you love." Thess said.

"You know how I feel about you. Why are you doing this?"

"Because I love you the same way. It feels like I can't breathe without you. She's just going to go back to cheating on you. Where is she when you need her the most Chelae? You're her option, but I choose you. What's it going to be? You with hamburger when you could have steak. When I made love to you that one time, oh my goodness."

"Don't go there please."

"Do you need me to come down there and tell her myself? You know what it is. I think you confused because she don't know what to do with all that that you working with. Put your clothes on and let me drive back to Shogun's, get some of that Garlic Shrimp you like. Then take a long drive to the Sinnissippi Gardens and put you on that bench again. You remember the bench right?"

"Yeah, I do."

"Has anyone ever made you feel like that? Don't lie Chelae."

"No."

"Good, meet me in lobby in an hour."

If you enjoyed this book, here are some other titles by Inakat you might also like:

Synz En Detroit

Sasha N. Deeplee

High Maintenance Assets

Coming 2013

Touch of Base

Synz Two: Remixed

@Inakat1 on Twitter

Inakat Detroit on Facebook

www.inakat.com

www.ingramcontent.com/pod-product-compliance
Lightning Source LLC
Chambersburg PA
CBHW060827120626
46557CB00001B/403